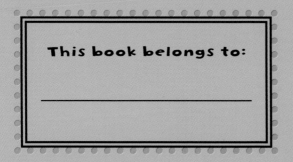

This book belongs to:

_____

A catalogue record for this book is available from the British Library
Published by Ladybird Books Ltd
80 Strand London WC2R 0RL
A Penguin Company
4 6 8 10 9 7 5 3
© Ladybird Books Ltd MMVI. This edition MMVIII

ISBN: 978-1-84646-986-2
Printed in China

The Magic Porridge Pot

Retold by Vera Southgate M.A., B.Com
with illustrations by Colin Sullivan

Ladybird *tales*

Once upon a time, there was a little girl who lived with her mother, who was a widow. They were so poor that one day they found they had nothing left to eat.

The little girl went off into the woods to play. She was so hungry that she began to cry. An old woman came up to her.

"Why are you crying, my child?" she asked.

"Because I am so hungry," said the little girl.

"Then you shall be hungry no more," said the old woman. She gave the little girl a small cooking pot.

Then the old woman said, "When you are hungry, just say to the pot, 'Cook, little pot, cook!' It will cook some very good porridge for you."

"When you want the pot to stop cooking," went on the old woman, "you must say, 'Stop, little pot, stop!'"

The little girl was so hungry that she wanted some porridge at once. So she said to the little pot, "Cook, little pot, cook!"

The little cooking pot did as it was told, and began to cook some porridge. The little girl could hardly wait to try some.

When the porridge was cooked, the little girl said, "Stop, little pot, stop!" The porridge tasted very good and the little girl ate every little bit of it.

The little girl ran home with the cooking pot to her mother, and told her what the old woman had said.

"Now our worries are over," said her mother happily. "The little pot will keep us well fed!"

Whenever they were hungry, they said to the cooking pot, "Cook, little pot, cook!"

The porridge was always very good, and they always enjoyed it.

One day the little girl went out for a walk. While she was out, her mother felt hungry. So she said, "Cook, little pot, cook!"

The pot began to cook some porridge. The mother began to eat it. It was very good porridge and she enjoyed it.

She was so busy eating the porridge that she forgot to tell the pot to stop cooking.

The pot went on and on, cooking more and more porridge.

Soon the porridge began to come over the top of the little cooking pot.

When the mother saw this, she knew that she must tell the pot to stop cooking. But she had forgotten the words!

The pot just went on and on, cooking more porridge. Soon there was porridge all over the table and all over the kitchen floor.

And still the little pot went on, cooking more and more porridge!

Soon all the house was full of porridge.

And still the little pot went on, cooking more and more porridge!

Soon the house next door was full of porridge.

And still the little pot went on, cooking more and more porridge!

Soon all the houses in the street were full of porridge.

And still the little pot went on, cooking more and more porridge!

Soon nearly all the streets in the town were full of porridge.

And still the little pot went on, cooking more and more porridge!

All the people, from all the houses, came out into the streets.

No one knew how to stop the little pot from cooking more porridge. It just went on and on, cooking more and more porridge.

The people in the town began to think that soon all the world would be filled with porridge.

Just as the porridge was reaching the last house in the town, the little girl came back from her walk.

At first, she could not tell what had happened to the town.

"Please stop the little pot from cooking any more porridge," cried her mother.

The little girl said, "Stop, little pot, stop!"

And then, at last, the little pot did stop cooking porridge.

But anyone who wants to go into that town now, will have to eat his way through a lot of porridge!